MY HIGH SCHOOL CHRISTMAS BOYFRIEND
A Sweet YA Holiday Romance

A boy

A dance

A disappearing act

A lost shoe

A wicked Great Aunt

There I was, starring in my very own fairytale, dancing with a handsome stranger at the Christmas Winter Dance.

But then, in a Cinderella reversal, *he was gone!*

And I was left musing over the boy who had set my heart on fire.

Can I find him again, and will I get my happy ending with the boy from the Christmas Dance?

Other books by Kylie Key

THE RIVER VALLEY HIGH BOYFRIEND SERIES

https://www.amazon.com/gp/product/B087KW9P14

My High School Fake Boyfriend - Maddie & Peyton

My High School Billionaire Boyfriend - Bella & Jack

My High School Rebel Boyfriend - Harper & Mitchell

My High School Royal Boyfriend - Blaire & Alexander

My High School Valentine Boyfriend - Shay & Finn

My High School Quarterback Boyfriend - Tanchia & Dean

My High School Secret Boyfriend - Saffron & Kyran

My High School Christmas Boyfriend - Rylee & Aiden

COVINGTON PREP: THE GIRLS WE LOVE

https://www.amazon.com/gp/product/B09KXFF5VM

The Tomboy - Taylor & Max

The Bookworm - Millie & Tennessee

The Kid Sister - Sierra & Cullen

The Heiress - Elisha & Phoenix

The Queen Bee - Bianca & Raine

The Celebrity - Tamsyn & Sloan

The Rebel - Valencia & Jade

The Wallflower - Izzy & Paris

THE YOUNG LOVE SERIES

https://www.amazon.com/gp/product/B08454JT1D

The Songs We Sing - Ella & Damon

The Path We Take - Dominique & Malachi

The Lies We Tell - Trieste & Felix

The Hearts We Break - Selina & Cole

The Dreams We Share - Ainsley & Logan
The Choices We Make - Damon
SWEET CRUSHES SERIES
https://www.amazon.com/dp/B0CW17BRVT
His Christmas Angel - Angelina & Chase
Cafe Crush - Evie & Taine

CONNECT WITH ME!
Check out my Amazon page here:
https://www.amazon.com/author/kyliekey
Join my newsletter here:
http://eepurl.com/dKX-A2

CHAPTER 1

AIDEN

I don't do dances. Like ever. They're just not me. Not Homecoming, not Sadie Hawkins, not Halloween. No thanks.

So I don't know why my two best friends, Vin and Harry are standing in my kitchen, eating slices of Mom's apple cake, discussing the Winter Dance as if I'm already going.

"You have to come," Vin says to me, but looking at my mother. "Tell him he's coming. It's a fundraiser you know."

The Winter Dance is being held on the last day of school, organized to raise funds for cancer research on behalf of Mrs. Phillips, an English teacher who has breast cancer.

I'm shaking my head, but Vin says, "I've already bought the tickets, Aiden." And with finality, "So we're going."

"You can pay Vin for the ticket," my mother orders me, and then in a soft tone, "How nice that they're fundraising. Such a good cause."

She offers glasses of juice, but Vin and Harry politely decline, as they always do. They know juice is a luxury in our house, that it's kept for visitors. They're not considered visitors.

Vin knuckle bumps us as if it's all settled, and then instructs Harry and me on when and where we'll meet. The dance is three days away, so I figure I have that much time to find a suitable excuse, or come down with the flu.

Like I said, I don't do dances.

I don't break my leg, my Grandma doesn't die, nor does the school gymnasium burn down, so as planned, Vin arrives in his truck. He has volunteered to do this because he is afraid I won't turn up if I'm left to my own devices. He grins and does a double take on my clothes, making out that seeing me in a button down shirt is a big deal.

"Looking sharp bro," he says and I ignore him, checking my hair in the hallway mirror as we leave. I push a few strands into place, my hand coming away sticky from the styling wax. My younger sister, Krystal waves from the living room, and when Mom remarks how handsome I look, Krystal nods vigorously. I go and hug her goodnight; it wastes a little more time.

We meet Jordy and Scott, Vin's football teammates in the parking lot; that's good, we're a crowd. The dance is in full-on mode and I position myself in the middle of the group, terrified that I'll be made to dance. I want to remain anonymous and well-blended, like a banana in a smoothie. You know it's in there, but you don't really see or taste it.

Jordy takes no time in making his move, he's been crushing on a girl called Kendall for months now, and with Scott in tow, they make their way to the dance floor. I keep close to Vin, best friend since middle school. He's a defensive back, and at six two and weighing close to two hundred pounds (which isn't all muscle), I feel sure there is no way he is going to be dancing. Not just sure, but confident.

So, along with Harry, who is the braniac of our group (he prefers that to nerd), and who hates the pop music that is playing more than I do, we discuss NBA scores, Mr Avery's pinstripe suit and Jordy's chances with Kendall.

And then, without any warning, Vin takes a step forward and says, "Come on boys, let's dance." And with the unexpected grace of a salsa dancer, he sashays onto the floor, a target obviously in his sights. A tall girl in a pale pink dress is smiling as if royalty is approaching, and Vin takes himself within inches of this girl, doing a cha cha cha in front of her. To say I'm stunned is an understatement, but there I am, next to him and Harry, now forced to make some sort of swaying move.

Awkward?

Uncomfortable?

Embarrassing?

Yep. All of the above.

Tall Girl is not on her own though, there are several girls around her, not that I look at any of them. At this stage I can only identify them by their shoes, because my eyes are firmly glued to the floor. There's a pair of high black sandals, a pair of gladiator type sandals, a pair of silver sandals with crystals hanging from them and a pair of black ankle boots.

The black ankle boots seem to be out of place and my eyes cast up the legs that are wearing the boots. The legs aren't very long, even with the dress being very short. The dress is a peachy color, there's a lacy bit at the top and it's sleeveless, which surprises me because it's the middle of winter. There's straight brown hair skimming along the bare shoulders and when my eyes finally lift up, they are met by dark brown eyes looking back at me.

And then a smile.

I smile back quickly, again embarrassed, and glance across to see Vin totally in Tall Girl's personal space, and Harry now pairing up with Gladiator Shoes. In the count of about ten seconds Black Sandals and Silver Crystal Sandals have faded into the background and somehow, by default, I am dancing (if you can call it that) with Ankle Boots.

Ankle Boots is still smiling and her arms are waving at her sides, she's tossing her hair around, all in time to the music. When the chorus comes on, she and everyone else in the room, except Harry and me (it seems), shout out the lyrics. Her hips are wiggling and her feet are tapping and I'm entranced by her. Her head rolls back, her arms shoot up and she shouts the words again. The smile on my face gets wider.

And then she grabs at my hands and pushes them overhead with hers, again shouting out the lyrics. I'm almost sorry when the song ends, but I needn't be. The next song starts up immediately, and again, she knows every word. A brief look over to Vin reveals him whispering into Tall Girl's ear and Harry is dancing in a robotic style which I hope is making my gentle bobbing look good.

Ankle Boots knows how to dance. Even with my limited knowledge and experience of girls and dances, I can tell this. Her hips are swinging seductively and I find myself unable to take my eyes off of her. In an unexpected move she takes my hand up high and twirls around under it, brushing against my chest as she does. I draw in a sharp breath and an unfamiliar tingle rushes through me. She reverses her twirl, this time her hair flicks across my chin. She smiles and then shouts out more words.

I have no idea who this girl is. In a school of two thousand students, that's not unusual, but I'm guessing she's a junior.

The song ends and Vin, to my horror is leading Tall Girl off the dance floor. Where on earth is he going? In desperation I search out Harry, relieved to see that his robot moves have just taken him a short distance behind me, both Gladiator Shoes and Silver Crystal Sandals in close proximity.

Ankle Boots is shouting something at me. I bend my head, but I frown at whatever she has said, going a little lower. The DJ has started the next song. Ankle Boots touches the side of my head, her mouth shouts in my ear, "What's your name? I'm Rydee." Her breath tickles my skin, again a tingle courses through my body.

For some reason I take hold of her face and turn her ear to me. She has four assorted earrings studded along the shell and I find myself shouting, "Rydee? I'm Aiden."

She grabs my ear again, "RyLEE," she shouts again, "RyLEE!"

I nod that I heard and she breaks into song again, apparently another favorite. She twirls and swivels, shakes and shimmies and my face feels tight from all the smiling I'm doing.

When it comes to an end she blows out her cheeks, "Wow, that's worked up a sweat!"

"You're getting a good workout," I say, noticing that the lights have dimmed and the first few bars of the next song start and everyone instantly falls silent. The slow beat isn't lost on me. I can be dense at times, and (it seems) this is one of them. Everyone who isn't slow dancing has already left the floor, the bodies around us have melded from two into one. Walking away now would make one conspicuous, and I don't want to be conspicuous.

Rylee is looking up at me. At the exact same time we step towards one another and my foot steps on hers.

"Sorry," I say, but she just chuckles and her arms reach out to go around my waist, and without realizing what I'm doing I'm pulling her towards me, my arms wrapping around her. Her head naturally falls onto my chest and our bodies move into a synchronized swaying, our feet not moving at all. For once she is quiet, she's not singing along at all, in fact nobody is. My hands are tense and rigid on her back; I'm in uncharted territory. Fearing my fingers are going to cramp, I shift them higher, getting the fright of my life as they move from fabric to bare skin. Seems there's a triangular hole in the back of her dress, and now I don't know what to do. My fingers freeze, but I'm burning up at the same time.

A girl I'd never seen until three songs ago is now the light of my life.

I'm suddenly wishing that the song never ends. But four minutes flashes by in a heartbeat and as the music stops, the lights shine back to full strength. Rylee's head lifts off my chest, my hands move back to touch her dress fabric, and our eyes connect.

I kiss her forehead. What. On. Earth.

She smiles, I smile.

"Shall we get a drink?" I ask, as the next song begins. She nods and I take her hand, leading her over to the refreshment tables, like I've been doing this my whole life. I haven't.

I down the fruity punch in one gulp and she looks at me with amusement, sipping daintily.

Gladiator Shoes and Silver Crystal Sandals approach us. They both look at me and I get a moment to register their faces. Gladiator has long, wavy black hair while Silver Crystal has short blonde hair with pink bits through it. They crowd Rylee, giggling in a girly way. She passes me her half full cup, shrugs her shoulders, laughing, "Won't be long," as her friends pull her away. I figure it's a girl thing.

I'm standing there scanning around for Harry when Scott comes bounding up to me, Harry close behind. He shoves me along, making me spill Rylee's punch on the floor.

"We need to get out of here," he says, "Jordy's about to get his head kicked in."

The three of us sweep up Vin on our way out, interrupting his extremely close encounter with Tall Girl. It seems that Kendall isn't as single as she thinks she is. Her former/current boyfriend has decided he's still in the picture. He's about to demonstrate to Jordy what this all means.

For a big guy Vin is pretty swift, and as he exhibited on the dance floor, light on his feet too. His size is intimidating, so he is the perfect ally in a situation like this. Typically, Scott, Harry and I are happy to let Vin take the lead. We'll be the back-up, though none of us are particularly suited to these situations. I'm a middle distance runner on the track team, Scott's a running back, while Harry's only sporting endeavours are on X-box.

Everything is a blur of shouting, threats and door slamming. Kendall and her girlfriend take off in her car. The ex points fingers at Jordy. Jordy jumps into his car, Vin joining him. Scott urges Harry and me to follow him to his car.

I have a split moment to make a decision. Go with my friends or go back to the dance. If I go back into the dance, I won't have a ride home. If I go with my friends I won't see Rylee again, and I don't have her number.

Harry, of all people, guides me to the car and my choices are voided. I settle in the back seat, bemoaning the fact that the best night of my life has just been cut short.

The Jordy/Kendall saga continues in the parking lot of Peppy's Pizza. Kendall's ex shows up with his posse and after a heated argument between him and Kendall and her bestie, he storms off in his Mustang, squealing tires adding to the drama. It's all stuff I'd rather not be a part of.

We grab a booth and pizzas are ordered and Vin becomes quite vocal about ditching the dance.

"Jeez Jordy," he is genuinely irritated, "I was just getting it on with Sacha, it was all happening."

Jordy has his arm around Kendall and just grins. "Sorry bro, I owe you." He looks at his watch. "Hey, there's still time to go back."

Vin just hmmphs, like it would be too much effort to go back, now that he's scoffing down pizza. I know that if I had my own car I'd drive him back. I'm cursing myself for not having it.

"Did you get her number?" Jordy asks.

"Yes, I got her number," Vin snaps, as if that's a given. Obviously I'm a fool for not getting Rylee's. The memory of my lips on her forehead and the feel of her skin jolts me and I look at my own phone for distraction.

"Who was the cutie you were with?" Harry asks, elbowing my side, almost making me drop my phone. Since when has Harry ever said the word *cutie*? Like, never.

I feel my cheeks redden and say, "Me? What about you? You had two of them."

"Aidy?" Jordy asks, and I hate that name, though it's better than being called Aids. "You were with a girl?" I don't know why there's so much astonishment is his voice. It's not like I'm a total loser. Or anything.

Harry laughs with a newfound sass I didn't know he possessed. "He was up close and personal!" This time I elbow his ribs and way harder than he did to me. He winces in pain; that pleases me.

"So, Aidy?" Jordy seems relentless in his questioning, which is odd because we're not best friends. "Spill, Aidy!"

"I don't know," I mutter, cheeks red-hot, "Rylee someone, I don't know." Then I add in an accusing tone, "Vin made us dance."

"Rylee *Martin*?" Jordy's eyes pop onto stalks.

His reaction instills a panic in me, like I have something to fear. Is she a weirdo? A freak? A juvie? Or worse, *popular*?

"You don't know Rylee Martin?" Jordy's face is tinged with amusement. I'm trying to appear unfazed, but I'm desperate to know more. Rylee Martin. Wicked dancer. Silky brown hair. Deliciously dark eyes. Perfectly kissable lips. Warm, soft skin.

Jordy's words make the blood drain from my body. "Her parents are Double A Developments. They practically *own* this town."

That means Rylee Martin is rich. Not rich. Very rich.

"Did you get her number? Did you get her number?" Harry is laughing now, razzing me, acting like a five year old.

I shake my head and shove him again. There's a collective murmur that this is probably a good thing, because it's obvious the story ends right here. Everyone knows that the fairytale of a school dance is one thing, the reality of life is another.

"So, what about the two girls you were dancing with?" Vin asks Harry. He gives me a wink, knowing I am loathing the attention.

Harry's bragging borders on fanciful, Jordy is locking lips with Kendall and Vin finishes the last slice of pizza. The topic of Rylee Martin is not resurrected. They know I have no chance with her.

Because, I'm Aiden Barrett, and I live in the poor part of town.

As soon as I get home, I search social media. Well, I am only human. Initially I don't find anything. Until I discover there are a hundred and one different ways to spell Rylee. I'd typed in Riley, then Rilee, then Ryleigh and so it went on. It's only after searching for Sacha (also spelt more than one way) that I finally find her.

All my fears are confirmed. Rylee Martin, junior, is out of my league.

Her dance moves, her smile, her hands around my waist, and the feel of her soft, warm skin under my lips are doomed to become nothing more than a distant memory.

CHAPTER 2

RYLEE

I'm glad I have already decided not to sleepover at Casey's house after the dance. Because what started out being the best day of my life has turned into the worst day of my life. And Casey, who is usually my best friend, feels like my worst friend.

She took me away from him.

The stranger I was dancing with.

I had no expectations for the Christmas Winter Dance, other than dancing the night away. The Halloween Dance had been a flop, the music had been disappointing, the band's sound system kept faltering, and my mermaid costume had been difficult to dance in because my high heels kept getting caught up in my long tail.

Casey and I had gone to Sacha's house to get ready. Two hours it took us, and even then we felt we were rushing. Our nails were painted, smudged and repainted. My hair was straightened and Sacha's was curled. Casey's short blonde do needed only to be blow dried and sprayed.

Our outfits were tried on, removed, swapped, on, off, on again. A collection of earrings, necklaces, bracelets, tried on, discarded, then reinstated. But while the others put on their heels, I wasn't going to make the same mistake twice. I was going to wear a pair of shoes that allowed me to dance. And if that that meant I'd look like a midget, especially next to Sacha, so be it. Like I said, I was there to dance.

We had arrived early, excitable juniors not worried about being un-cool, but keen to support the breast cancer charity and have a night of fun. Sacha, though, had high hopes that her weeks of flirting with Vin Trembolton, football star *and* senior, would finally come to fruition. At

14

five eleven, Sacha towers over most of the boys in our year, but Vin Trembolton is a solid six two.

Sacha's coy glances to the perimeter were soon rewarded when, like a scene from High School Musical, the crowd parted and Vin approached her, flanked by two other boys. As the rest of us, Casey, Bree, Aliyah and me gawked and giggled, I found one of the boys dancing right in front of me. I thought it was a random positioning as they tried to fit onto the crowded dance floor, but he stayed facing me, though his eyes were focused downward.

As if he had been studying his footwork, he slowly raised his eyes. That's when I expected that he would swing around, realizing he was in the wrong place, with the wrong girl. Surely he would prefer Casey or Bree, both of them of a more reasonable height. Stupid me, I cursed myself for choosing comfort over fashion!

I smiled at him, instantly drawn to his dreamy eyes, framed by long fluttering eyelashes which made me jealous—no doubt his weren't fake extensions like my own. His brown hair flopped across his forehead like a shield that he wanted to hide behind. His cheekbones were visible, envious angles that my blusher could never achieve. I wanted to grab his defined jaw and tilt his head back so I could get lost in his colorless eyes.

Surprisingly, he smiled back, his eyes connecting for only a moment before he once again examined the floor. Looking down, I saw his black Converse were well scuffed, well worn. Well, we had that in common, comfort first!

Certain that he would make a dash for it when there was a break in the music, I put in my best moves. May as well try to impress him. If not, hopefully Misty van der Weghe, queen-of-the-junior-year and already-in-the-senior-cheer-squad, would see me dancing with a senior.

Two songs later, and Mr Good Looking Senior was still dancing with me. At one point Casey caught my eye and winked, but I'd let my inhibitions run free and was singing my heart out. Mr GLS wasn't singing, but he was smiling. As the second chorus rolled around I sang even louder, making him laugh, and as everyone around us was throwing their arms in the air, I grabbed his hands, thrusting them above us. He didn't pull away, no he stretched our arms even higher.

Okay, surely after that song he'd had enough. Vin had his arm on Sacha's shoulder, he was guiding her through the crowd, off the dance floor. Surely that was Good Looking Senior's cue to depart. Spontaneously, I went up on tiptoe and said, "What's your name? I'm Rylee." He didn't understand. I shouted louder, right into his eardrum.

Then he leant down, touched my face. "Rydee?" he said in a slightly husky voice, as if he needed a drink. "I'm Aiden."

Rydee? I had almost burst out laughing. "RyLEE. RyLEE," and he nodded.

My spirits had been high right then. I knew his name, and he knew mine. It was the third song and he was still with me. Rylee Martin, junior, was rocking it with a senior!

"Wow, that's worked up a sweat," I said, as the song came to an end, hoping my deodorant was doing its job.

"You're getting a good workout," he smiled, and still he didn't move. Didn't say thanks for the dance and disappear. I scouted the room, a back up plan in place in case I was suddenly a group of one.

There was a delay of several seconds before I recognized the next song as being a ballad. Oh my goodness, perhaps he didn't know. He hadn't sung any lyrics up to now, so he was probably clueless. We were going to look like total idiots dancing separately when everyone around us was making out. If he lead me off the dance floor in the next two seconds we might avoid embarrassment.

Time was up. I took a step forward, encouraging him to escort me away with at least an ounce of dignity. He stepped toward me, landing on my toe. We both shuffled our feet and laughed and somehow our arms went around each other, my head resting on his chest. I could smell him, the faint scent of Axe spray on his shirt, and even though I should have been nervous, I wasn't. His hands moved across my back, his fingertips gliding on my skin, and still there were no nerves. Everything felt so right. Even though we had only exchanged a couple of sentences, nothing about being in his arms felt awkward. And, as his body rocked against mine, his touch making my heartbeat accelerate, still it didn't feel wrong.

I dreaded the song finishing, I wanted it to be on repeat, so Aiden couldn't free me from his embrace, but the last piano note died and he drew back from me as the lights powered up, the chaperones circling with their phone torches. It was then that I noticed his eyes were in fact light hazel, maybe Pinterest would call them amber.

As I mentally prepared myself to be separated from him, his hands stroked my hair and he kissed my forehead. My eyes closed as his lips lingered, *I'm never washing my forehead again!*

And when they opened, he was smiling at me. "Do you want to get a drink?" he asked, and pulled me by the hand to where chaperones were serving fruit punch.

He drank his cup quickly and was about to say something when Casey and Ailyah surrounded me, Casey's eyebrows raising and Ailyah's head motioning toward the restrooms.

"Won't be a minute," I said, and he took my cup from me. Casey and Ailyah giggled all the way to the restroom and the conversation was full of *Oh Mys* and *Go Girl,* as I verified everything they'd just witnessed. Our excitement, and it was a joint effort, couldn't be contained.

Casey and Ailyah double checked my hair and my lipstick and I walked back into the hall full of confidence. But my heart sank when we could see that Aiden wasn't where we had left him. My eyes desperately searched the room, once, twice, three times.

Stupid. That's what I was. Stupid. Leaving a hot guy for a bathroom break that I hadn't even needed. Talking myself up about having hooked a senior. A senior who had slow danced with me and kissed my forehead.

I felt my chin tremble as the truth became obvious. Aiden was gone. Four songs of politeness and then he'd disappeared as soon as I was out of sight. I sucked in my lips, trying to control my emotion.

"Hey, let's dance," Casey said, her hand on my back and her head leaning on mine. That was when she felt like my worst and best friend. She'd taken me away from Aiden, but she was also my shoulder to cry on. I followed her and Ailyah back to the dance floor, pretending that I didn't care about the last twenty minutes of my life. Better to forget it ever happened.

"SO, HOW WAS THE DANCE?" Mom asks.

"Good," I say, my eyes staring vacantly out as we drive home. There is a little consolation in knowing that the long-haired boy ditched too, and that Vin also dashed off, though Sacha has given him her number. Perhaps they came as one ride, I convince myself, perhaps they have a curfew, perhaps they are leaving town on vacation. And perhaps the moon is made of cheese.

"Did you dance with anyone special?" Mom is subtly prying.

"Mainly the girls."

"Did Sacha get her man?" Mom laughs. There has been no secret about Sacha's crush.

"Yes, and she gave him her number." I sound bitter and jealous. That's because I am.

"Oh?" Mom has sensed it.

I take in a deep breath, unable to contain myself for a second longer. "A boy did dance with me. One of Vin's friends. But he disappeared when I went to the bathroom."

"Oh," Mom says, and then she stutters, obviously rethinking what she was about to say. "Um, did you get his name?"

"Aiden. But he's a senior."

"Mmmm," Mom muses. "That's probably a good thing then. He'll be off to college before you know it." She has already declared the relationship doomed. "I hope Sacha doesn't get heartbroken."

It's when I'm in bed that a text comes from Sacha: that Vin and his friends had to go and help another of their friends who was about to get into a fight.

My heart bursts and sings with hope. Maybe Aiden was forced to depart quickly, perhaps he didn't mean to abandon me. And most of all, perhaps that forehead kiss wasn't meaningless.

CHAPTER 3

AIDEN

I have some work at the Christmas tree farm for the next week. It's physical, helping people load trees onto their cars and trailers, but it's also mentally draining, listening to them select their perfect tree. There are so many details people seem to care about when choosing a tree, they argue over height, branch placement, needle retention, fragrance and greenness. Still, it's worth putting up with for the pay packet.

I wish the world didn't revolve around money. But, I guess only people who don't have money say that. People with money say it's not important, but that's because, whether they recognize it or not, money has put them into the position where they are able to say that.

I have a vague memory of living in a big, two level brick house with a yard out the back and a basketball hoop in the driveway. That was back when Krystal was a baby. When my Dad was still alive. He died suddenly from a brain aneurysm, literally talking and breathing one minute, the next comatose on the living room floor. I had jumped on him, thinking he wanted a wrestling match. I'd pummeled his chest and declared victory.

There had been twenty four hours of hope, and then the unimaginable bombshell that he was brain dead and that Mom should turn off his life support.

I was ten at the time, and that memory replays over and over. It haunts me that I didn't know he was unconscious, that I should've called for help earlier. Mom says it would have made no difference to the outcome, but *what if*...?

All I know is that anyone can die, anywhere, at any time.

What I do remember is moving into the house we live in now. We've been here six years. It's a square box with a single garage and the backyard looks into the neighbor's kitchen window. They're an older couple who are very friendly, so there's that, I guess. There are a lot of elderly people in the neighborhood, which Mom likes. She feels safe here. She says it's a good place for Krystal to grow up.

It's the expected frantic, last minute rush of tree shoppers, but I breeze through it, Rylee Martin in my thoughts the whole time, her magical laugh, her swinging hair, her soft skin. I have good intentions of asking Vin to find out more about her. But I know I won't, *I just imagine that I will.* It's that sort of false faith that you have in yourself that keeps you going, that gives you hope.

Vin has already asked Sacha to the movies tonight. I'm in awe of his confidence. Whereas I'm going to daydream about Rylee Martin until I graduate, Vin is out there making things happen.

Harry and Scott invite themselves around in the evening. No one minds coming to my house, even though it's further away and a lot smaller than everyone else's. Maybe they like the intimacy. We have to game in the living room where Krystal will usually be sitting or playing, and Mom is always within earshot at the kitchen table where she reads or bakes or does craft work.

Tonight the house smells like gingerbread because she's making a batch of candles to sell at the Christmas Markets. It's a little sideline she does to make a bit of extra money, in addition to working in the office at Krystal's school. Basically, she has never spent a day apart from Krystal since her birth; her choice.

"Mrs B, they smell good enough to eat," Harry says, rocking up with bags of snack food and cans of energy drinks. He's anticipating a long night, obviously forgetting I have work tomorrow. "You'll put aside two for Mom and Khloe, won't you. I'll pay you next week."

"Don't be silly," Mom says. "If you want some, just take them." As far as she's concerned my friends are family.

"No way," Harry says. "Can you gift wrap them for me? Are you making gingerbread cookies this year, too?"

Mom smiles. "Yes, I'll be baking tomorrow."

"Good!" Harry smiles and rubs his hands together. "I'll order a box of those too!" At Halloween he ordered several boxes of Mom's Eyeball and Severed Finger cookies for trick or treaters. Harry's parents are both lawyers; his Mom worked with my Dad, who was in the police force. His loyalty to my family is fierce.

We settle in for a typical night of gaming, the distraction temporarily takes my mind off of Rylee. That is until Harry, out of the blue, says, "Would I have a chance with Ailyah?"

"She ditched you, didn't she?" Scott offers no empathy, not one ounce. "You forced yourself on her, didn't you?" I, in the meantime, shrug.

"I didn't *force* myself," Harry insists, "we were dancing and she gravitated towards me."

"Gravitated?" Scott isn't convinced.

"Yeah, she kinda moved in my direction."

"Really?"

"Come on, support me here Aidy," Harry tosses his controller onto the floor and grabs the packet of chips. "She was drawn to me."

"Possibly," I say, non-committal.

"Thought you said you were dancing with two girls," Scott says. If there's a hole in the story, he'll sniff it out.

"Yeah, Ailyah, and then Casey joined us," Harry says. "They both wanted me."

"Whatever," Scott scoffs. "More likely one was trying to save the other from you. That's what girls do, Harry."

"If Jordy didn't need our help, it'd be a completely different story," Harry shoves chips into his mouth, preferring to live in his own fantasy world. He has about as much chance of hooking up with Ailyah as I have of asking Rylee Martin out. Zero. Zilch. A big fat 0.

Our phones ping simultaneously, and we all cackle as we open the picture Vin has sent. He's outside Sacha's house, the camera recording the front path to her door, stopping as he's about to knock.

"He's doing it," Scott says, his voice swelling with pride. "Vin is doing it!"

Harry and I nod, in awe and amazement. Yes, Vin is doing it, and Harry and I aren't. And probably never will.

On the day after meeting Rylee, I can't remember if she comes up to my chin or my nose.

On the second day of not seeing Rylee, I'm not sure whether her hair is shoulder length or longer.

On day three, I've forgotten if she has three or four earrings in each ear.

It's three days before Christmas and it's been raining on and off, so Mr Bruce, the boss let's me go home early. It pleases Mom because it means I can watch Krystal while she gets herself organized for the night market. Me, not so much, it's money I'm not going to earn. I don't like asking Mom for money, her whole life is on a tight budget, and I'd really like to help out more.

The house is warm from the smells of vanilla and cinnamon as Mom finishes packaging cookies into gift boxes. There seem to be an awful lot of them.

"You think you'll sell them all?" I ask.

"I sold out last year, so I'd rather have too many," she says. "If there are leftovers I'll take them with us to the Christmas lunch."

"That's if I don't eat them first," I say with a laugh.

"I've kept you some broken ones," Mom says, ruffling my hair as she directs me to stack the boxes into her utility cart. "And if it doesn't rain again, how about taking Kryssie to see the Christmas lights? Maybe drive around St Mark's? Mrs Baker says the houses are beautiful."

"Okay," I say. St Mark's is the posh neighborhood, it's not far away in distance, down the road and up a steep, windy hill, but in house values, it's a million miles away. I help her load up her minivan, and she leaves me with a list of instructions for Krystal. It's not like she needs to, but it gives her peace of mind.

"I'll be home around nine. Unless I sell out," she says, smiling and tapping on the door frame.

"Yeah, good luck. Though you don't need it."

"Mrs Baker is home, if you need anything." She nods across to our next door neighbor's house and draws my attention to the note she's written.

"Mom," I say firmly, "we'll be fine." She has a contingency plan in place for every possible scenario, including an earthquake. Our state is not known for its earthquakes.

"Well, call me if you need anything. And wrap Kryssie up warm if you do go out. Her jacket is in the-"

"Mom, I know where Kryssie's jacket is," I shout as I shoo her away with my hands. She ducks into the living room, hugging Krystal, who waves enthusiastically.

I go back into the kitchen, munching on the reject cookies, and peruse the list, pleased to see that Krystal doesn't need a bath tonight and that Mom's left a lasagna in the oven to reheat. That will give me plenty of time to wrap the presents I've brought, and I'll be able to get Krystal into bed and sit and watch the basketball game.

I pour myself a glass of water, checking out the window. The rain clouds have blown away and it has turned into a decent evening, but it's only going to get colder. In a spur of the moment decision, I go into the hallway closet and retrieve Krystal's jacket, her Little Red Riding Hood coat, I call it.

"Hey," I bound into the living room, shaking it in front of her, "let's go for a drive?" If I can get the lights out of the way, I can get her settled for the night early.

She smiles and nods, slowly sits herself up and sheds the blanket she's under. She waits for me to help her stand up and holds her arms out so I can put her jacket on. My sister is ten years old, looks about six and has the brain capacity of a two year old. She was brain damaged at birth, a delivery botch-up that resulted in an emergency C-section, her life saved, but the injury permanent.

To a stranger she initially looks normal, she's pretty with her light brown colored eyes and fair hair which she loves to wear in two long braids. But she's very thin and it's her hands that give away her disability, her fingers always stiff and at unnatural angles, and when she walks she drags one foot.

Her speech is limited, but she seems to understand more than she can speak. She'll forever wear diapers and won't learn to read or write, but she loves Dora the Explorer and Frozen until it drives me and Mom insane. Her laughter is a magical sound.

"We'll go and see some lights, and some Christmas trees." I zip her up, gather her beanie, gloves and shoes which Mom has tidily put aside. She jiggles excitedly as she realizes that we're going out, making me smile. It also makes me wonder what goes on inside that brain of hers. Is the mere thought of an outing enough to ignite such joy in a person?

Mind you, I can answer that. The mere thought of one day seeing Rylee Martin again triggers that same kind of response.

With her all wrapped up, I grab my keys, but Krystal is standing at the door with her scooter. "We're going in the car," I say, but there's no point in repeating myself. If Krystal thinks she's scootering, then she's scootering. I follow her out to the gate, buckle her into her car seat, then put the scooter in the trunk.

It gets dark early these days, but it's still an hour until sunset. I'm praying that the posh houses have their lights on already. Surely they don't have to worry about their electric bills. Their flashing reindeer and sleighs and Santas will be ostentatiously displayed in their yards. Driving around St Mark's can be a stark reminder of excess opulence and an unkind lesson in mankind's obsession with material affluence. For me, but not for Krystal—she just likes to see all things sparkly and twinkly.

I drive down a street slowly, pointing out the pretty lights, the garish, over-the-top scenes, the huge trees, but I feel conspicuous. My Honda, that's older than me, sticks out like a sore thumb in this neighborhood. People are going to think I'm casing the place, they're going to be peering out from behind their luxury blinds, ready to push their security alarms or call the police. I park the car at the end of a street and pull the scooter out. The girl was a genius to bring it—we'll do a walk around the block and look like any kid and his sister looking at the decorations.

Krystal's scootering is a slow effort, but I'm not bothered, after all it is Christmas. Krystal stops and looks at every house, her eyes beaming at the excessive amount of colorful fairy lights. The string I hung under our front eaves seems pretty basic in comparison, but it still delights Krystal. It shames me that I haven't done much with her lately, that I've been too focused on exams, and work, and that stupid Christmas Dance.

It would take me about four minutes to walk to the end of the street, but fifteen minutes later we finally get there, and I'm grateful no other pedestrians are around. I guess everybody is caught up in last minute shopping or tucked up inside their warm homes.

"Are you tired?" I ask, and knowing I won't get an answer, continue, "Do you think you can go all the way around the block?" I figure that will make us look less like stalkers. I assist her to steer her clunky scooter—it's not the standard two wheeled kind, but has three for better balance. We turn the corner and she carries on at her snail pace, stopping at every gate. I follow, an eye on her, one checking basketball scores on my phone.

She comes to a halt outside a grand house with perfectly manicured shrubs that are blinking with golden lights. But Krystal is drawn to the front window where a massive tree is decorated in a silver and pink color scheme, like it's straight out of a shopping mall. Of course Krystal loves everything pretty and pink. She can't point because both hands are firmly gripping the scooter, but I can see she's mesmerized by the flashing lights. I see movement through the window and encourage Krystal to keep moving. Don't want to be accused of loitering.

I hear the click of the door as it opens and as I push Krystal forward, a voice calls, "Hey," and I turn around, already in defensive mode, to find that standing at the front of the house is Rylee Martin.

CHAPTER 4

RYLEE

I'm calling it fate. I'm on the couch watching the original Home Alone movie for the umpteenth time. It's three days till Christmas and I'm done with shopping. I've been at the mall with Casey all morning, a headache now kicking in, which has made me cancel plans to join her and Sacha at the night markets. Because lying horizontal on the couch is much more appealing. And I have my Great Aunt Patty fussing over me like I'm one step away from death's door. And I'm milking it. I haven't had to move a muscle as she's been delivering me Advil, hot chocolate and fresh baked cookies on request.

I feel a little guilty, but only a little. It's been a frantic semester, with junior exams and dance rehearsals and volleyball and falling in love.

Well, I'm being a bit dramatic, but since I was kissed on the forehead I've been emotionally drained, a wreck, his lips, his face, his hands consuming my every waking moment. If that's what love is, I'm in it. Head over heels. It feels wonderful and scary and awesome, but because I haven't seen him again, it's also exhausting and worrying and devastating.

Sacha is going through the same thing. Well, the first part of my list, the wonderful, scary and awesome part. But she has actually snared the boy and has been on a date, and texts and calls him and has bought him a Christmas gift. My date and conversations with Aiden are all in my head, and my gift is imaginary (an elf hat for fun and a bottle of fancy cologne, because he seems like the kind of boy who should wear a scent called *One Million.*)

All the girls keep asking if I've heard from him, and I have to say no and pretend I don't care, because rejection, I am learning, hurts. First, they tried to convince me that he's probably gone away on vacation. But then Sacha heard from Vin that he was working at the Christmas tree farm. So, that, in a way, filled me with hope. He was too busy working to ask for my number, so other than go buy a Christmas tree I don't need, I'm not sure how to hunt him down.

And that's when fate intervenes.

Bubbles, my cat, who is nestled on my hip, makes a sudden leap and stalks over to the window, something having caught his eye.

"Ooh, careful," Great Aunt Patty cries, knitting up a storm in the recliner. It's a scarf for Dad, one he'll never wear. "Rylee take him away from the tree or it'll come tumbling down."

I sigh as I get up. Aunt Patty is staying with me while my parents are on a Caribbean cruise. It happens every year just before Christmas. They get a week in the sunshine as a reward for their hard work throughout the year; I get Aunt Patty, a bitter spinster who delights in bossing me and Bubbles around. Since my grandmother, Mom's mother, passed away three years ago, Aunt Patty, who has never been married (never dated, I'd bet), has taken it on herself to be her replacement.

"Bubbles," I growl, dropping to my hands and knees, to lure him back. You would have thought from the amount of times he gets told off, he would learn not to go near it. He has certainly learned to keep well away from Aunt Patty, who sits on *his* recliner.

Bubbles ventures into the corner and I crawl up behind, ready to swoop on him. But my heart lurches as I look up to see Aiden Barrett standing outside my house. I mean, he's wearing a black jacket and the hood is up, but I think I'd know the face of the boy who kissed my forehead. I freeze, as he's looking straight through the window, and for a moment it feels like all my dreams are coming true. Even though he abandoned me at the dance, and has made no attempt to contact me, a minor miracle has had him search for me, like Prince Charming searching for Cinderella.

He is standing no more than thirty feet from my front door, and in my head, he is about five seconds away from pressing the doorbell.

But my dream is quickly destroyed when I see a young girl on a scooter come up alongside him. The girl stops and looks at our tree, the pink and silver lights flashing intermittently, putting on a mini lightshow.

Aiden points. I flatten myself to the floor, trying to conceal myself. I don't want to be caught spying. Like a worm, I shuffle backwards on the floor, rising onto my knees when I'm behind the safety of the branches.

"Rylee, what are you doing?" Aunt Patty tuts. I glance around, but can't see Bubbles. Aiden has one hand on the scooter as the little girl points. At me? At the tree? I rearrange a few baubles.

"What are you doing?" This time Aunt Patty snaps.

"There's someone out there," I whisper, peering out. They haven't moved. The girl is smiling.

Aunt Patty's hearing must be sharp, because she barks, "Well, stay away from the window. The security alarms are on."

Aiden gestures and the girl gets the scooter moving. My heart lurches and I spring up. Now or never. An opportunity.

I dash out the front door wearing unicorn socks, the sound of my own blood rushing in my ears, muffling out Aunt Patty's cry of, "Where are you going?"

"Hey," I call.

He turns, his eyes widening in shock. He steps into the path of the scooter to stop it, then looks back to me. "Rylee?"

"Hi." I wave my fingers at him in a cutesy way. He obviously hasn't hunted me down. His appearance here, outside my house, is totally random.

"What are-?" I ask at the same time that he says, "Do you-?"

We both quit talking, the silence strained for a moment as I take the time to breathe in deeply, to normalize my blood flow, but the smile that creeps on my face—I can't stop that.

CHAPTER 5

AIDEN

Upon hearing the door open, my apology is ready: *No, sorry, we weren't trying to peep in your window, my sister was smitten by your amazing display of Christmas decorations and lights.*

But I do a double take. It isn't an old person about to bite our heads off, but Rylee Martin appears in front of me like an apparition, looking ethereal in a white lacy sweater, pale blue leggings and colorful socks.

"Rylee?" I put my phone in my pocket and stop Krystal's scooter. The shock of seeing her makes me flustered. But should I be surprised? I'm walking down one of the swankiest streets in town—did my subconscious know that she might live here? "Hey." I want to go over to her, but Krystal won't be able to turn so quickly. "Do you-?" I start to say, and she, too, stops mid-sentence.

And then silence.

"Hey, my sister was just admiring your Christmas tree." I forget what I was going to ask her. "She's fascinated by the lights." I'm aware she's probably mad at me for ditching her at the dance and I prepare myself to be verbally assaulted.

Krystal tries to make a move, so I put my hand up in a stop gesture.

Rylee takes a step towards us. And my heart races as I see that her hair is lighter than I remembered, shades of brown and blonde, and it's not dead straight, but softly wavy, the kind you want to rub your nose in, and I'm imagining it smells like chocolate. Though I'm not sure chocolate has a distinctive smell. She looks even prettier in natural light, if that's at all possible, her lips curling up into a wide smile.

I don't want her to be mad at me and I blurt out in a panic, "Hey, I'm really sorry about the dance."

31

"Sorry for?" she asks.

It feels like a trick question. "You know, just disappearing like that. But there was an emergency with my friend-" She cuts me off.

"It's okay. Sacha told me all about it." She's smiling, so that's a good thing.

"Oh, cool," I say, "I was kinda stressing about it. I didn't want you to think I was a jerk."

"I was kinda hoping you weren't," she says, "a jerk, that is."

We're both looking at each other and I can feel I have this stupid grin on my face. What is it about this girl that sends my body into an internal frenzy? That has my heart doing flips and my cells excreting buckets of adrenaline, as if it's a life or death situation. For a moment I forget that I have Krystal with me. Until she shakes the scooter handles.

"Do you want to bring her in to see the tree?" Rylee asks, bending down to Krystal's level. "Do you want to come in?"

Krystal has a cute little smile on her face which makes me want to pick her up and squeeze her tight. That's my protective, big brother side.

"She doesn't speak," I say quietly, not wanting to embarrass Rylee. I like the fact that she's put the effort in to talk directly to Krystal. Not many people do that.

"Oh," Rylee says, unflappable, standing back to full height, which is a tad below my shoulders. "Can I show her the tree?"

"Dah-rink," Krystal says, making a liar of me. There are a list of words she can say, most related to food.

"Oh, I think she wants a drink," I say, "I better get her home."

Rylee looks up at me as if I'm crazy. She takes Krystal by the hand, "We can go inside for a drink then. What's her name?"

"Krystal," I say, and I'm left holding the scooter. "Hey, I don't think it's a good idea..."

"Why not? She'll love it." She looks at me with a defiant stare on her face. But there's a glint in her eye, a tilt of her head, a slight curve of her lips, which sets my heart on fire, which has me remembering that forehead kiss. And when her eyes scan across my face, I get the feeling she's remembering it too. It doesn't matter that her parents are billionaires and mine sells cookies to make ends meet. She pulls Krystal along, which sends my heart surging again. "How old is she?"

"Ten, she's ten," I say, trying to catch up. I prop the scooter against the wall, anxiety taking over—Krystal could be unpredictable in an unfamiliar setting. She might shake and cry and need implicit consoling.

"Ten? Ooh, you're like a little fairy, aren't you?" Rylee says. Likely she has no idea what Rylee is saying, but Krystal's laughter rings out like a heavenly choir. Rylee leads us up the path to the open door and her voice drops to a whisper. "My aunt is inside, she's a bit grumpy." But she says it with a smile.

I bend down and try to quickly untie my boots, struck by the thought that I'm probably wearing odd socks. My fingers tangle in the laces and I end up kicking them off. Rylee is leading Krystal into the living room.

"Hey, hey, hey, Kryssie. Shoes," I call. The entranceway is polished wood, but I can see her headed to an alarmingly pristine, light-colored carpet.

Krystal ignores me, the lure of lights a magnet for her. In mismatched socks, I slide and scoop her up on the precipice of the luxurious flooring, saving it from muddy footprints. I crouch with her on my knee, pulling off her purple sneakers. At least her striped socks *are* a pair.

"Need to take your shoes off in a new place," I say into her ear, "and don't touch anything."

The look on Krystal's face when she sees the living room is pure joy. The Martins obviously put a lot of effort into the holiday season and the house is like Santa's personal grotto. My Mom is mad on Christmas, and the fairy lights have been up since November but this house is a masterclass, like it could be featured in House and Garden. The tree is displayed in the center of the window, the decorations precise and balanced, nothing random here. There are beautiful stockings hanging on the mantlepiece, everything co-ordinated in pink and silver. The place reeks of luxury and sophistication and I feel significantly inferior. Especially wearing one black sock and one gray sock, which has multiple holes.

An old lady has risen from her recliner, shedding a soft mustard-colored blanket. Her droopy eyes are framed by finely arched eyebrows, her white hair pulled back in a severe bun, her face lined and hard, her expression stern and dour.

"Who is this?" she asks, like she's the Queen of England, her tone implying we're unfit peasants. Her steely eyes follow Krystal, who is making a beeline to a side table where a motorized Santa Sleigh is going round and round a loop track.

"Aunt Patty, this is my friend Aiden, from school," Rylee says, taking on her own British accent, "and his sister, Krystal." I'm interested in the fact that she has labeled me a friend. Probably sounds better than *Boy who dumped me at the dance.*

"*Don't* touch that," Aunt Patty bellows, ignoring the introduction. But Krystal is oblivious to the instruction or tone. She is completely captivated by the circling sleigh and will contentedly watch it for the rest of the evening, if she's able. The smallest, simplest things make her happy, it's both wondrous and heart-breaking.

"I said *don't* touch it," Aunt Patty repeats, "it's worth a lot of money."

"She's not touching it, Aunt Patty," Rylee says, releasing a frustrated breath, "she's just looking at it."

"It's worth a lot of money," Aunt Patty says again, "it was made in Switzerland." The crispness of her words implies I don't know where Switzerland is.

"We really should go," I say to Rylee, crouching down to Krystal and wrapping my arm around her shoulder, "let's go, Angel."

"No, let me get her a drink first," Rylee says. "She's thirsty."

"No, she'll be fine. I'll get her home," I say, aware that Aunt Patty is glaring disapprovingly at my feet. I try to wriggle my sock to conceal the hole by my big toe. I scoop Krystal into my arms and settle her on my hip. She writhes and whines, reaching her hand towards Rylee, as if she needs saving.

"Yes, this isn't exactly a place for children," Aunt Patty says, looking down her thin nose at us, "especially children like *that*."

My heart hammers, my chest tightens and my hands quiver. It's a reaction I've experienced many times—when the ugly voice of prejudice raises its head. People who vocally express their ignorance to my sister's condition, who judge and discriminate and practice intolerance. Mom has taught me to walk away in silence, to not answer back. It's hard sometimes, so hard, but I know it's the right thing to do this time. I head towards the door, sorry that I've subjected Krystal to this humiliation, even though she has no idea. *But I know.*

"Aunt Patty..." Rylee throws me a look of genuine distress. I love her for it. "Aunt Patty, Krystal isn't-"

"There's a *place* for children," Aunt Patty says through tight lips, lifting her chin in an arrogance that makes my heart slump.

I bend down and grab Krystal's sneakers and tuck them under my arm, then I shove my feet into my boots, the left one refusing to go in properly, but good enough that I can walk.

"Aiden," Rylee is by my side, "Aiden, I'm so sorry. You don't need to go. Aunt Patty is just an old-" Her eyes are watering, and Krystal's arm is flailing in her direction.

"Rylee! Close that door," Aunt Patty shouts, "there's a draft coming in!"

"I'm really, really sorry, I didn't know she'd-"

"It's okay," I murmur. "It's not your fault." It's *my* fault. For a stupid second I thought that it didn't matter that I'm from a poor, single-parent family, that I live in the Flats, that my sister has a disability.

But it does.

Those things matter.

To people like this.

People like Rylee's family.

I pick up Krystal's scooter with my fingertips and flee.

CHAPTER 6

RYLEE

I slam the door, my breath coming in gasps, my vision blurring from the mounting tears.

"RYLEE!" Aunt Patty's ear-blasting screech makes me shudder. "We don't close doors like that!"

I try to gather strength in my legs, beg my body to co-operate, will my chin to stop quivering. I have never felt so ashamed in my whole sixteen years. Never felt so weak, so useless. So angry.

I suck oxygen into my lungs, sniff and rub the corners of my eyes. I step back into the living room, Aunt Patty standing tall by the tree, peering out to check that Aiden and Krystal have left the premises.

"You can't just invite any riff-raff into your house, Rylee." Her face is etched with a cold-heartedness I've never witnessed before. Oh, Aunt Patty is gruff, she barely cracks a smile, but as the founder of her own sporting goods company back in the day, fighting as a single woman in a male dominated industry, she's had to be tough.

And though she can come across as posh and standoffish, in an obscure way she has always shown me affection and been tremendously generous. So this frank and cruel outburst has been a deplorable revelation.

And it's totally unforgivable.

I try to speak, but I'm having trouble breathing. I'm having trouble thinking.

"Rylee, what are you so upset about?" Her tone has sunk to bitter sarcasm. "He's not from up here, is he?"

By *up here*, she means St Mark's, the exclusive suburb where the rich and the powerful and privileged live, where I live. Anywhere else is unfit for human habitation.

"Just look at his clothes." She's so unkind, I feel nauseous. "Who would wear socks with holes in them? And odd socks at that," she huffs. "A boy has to have personal standards, Rylee." She sniffs in a breath. "Oh yes, I saw the way you looked at him. And the way he was looking at you. Nothing escapes me, my dear," she says with the smugness of a parent who has some gossip to share.

My lips pucker and twitch, my brain is ready to explode, though I'm intrigued—what does she mean by *the way he was looking at you?*

"Socks!" I shout, "they're just socks. What does it matter what kind of socks a person wears? They're just socks!"

Aunt Patty looks aghast, but her voice is calm and condescending, speaking to me like I'm a child. "Manners, Riley. No need for tantrums."

I stare her down, my eyes watering again, and no matter how hard I try to squeeze them away, the tears come. "No wonder you've never been married," I shout, "you're a selfish, horrible person who's all alone!"

Aunt Patty shows no emotion. "I'll get started on dinner," she says curtly, promptly turning and leaving the room, denying me the chance of a dramatic exit. I bound up the stairs to my room, burying myself under my covers, clinging to my childhood teddy bear, Bluey.

It's times like this that I miss Mom, and can't wait for her return tomorrow.

I send her a text: *Love you, can't wait to see you xx*

Her reply: *Looking forward to coming home, early flight, be back just after lunch, love you too darling. Hope you're behaving for Aunt Patty!*

I type: *I hate Aunt Patty*

But I backspace, realizing that the issue isn't my feelings for my aunt, the issue is the way Aiden and his sister were treated. Aunt Patty showed her true colors, her despicable views of intolerance against...I'm not even sure what—is it Krystal's disability or that Aiden lives in the wrong area? Or is it as simple as hating on a boy who wears mismatched socks?

I knew Aiden didn't live in St Mark's. My amateur sleuthing (which means questioning Sacha, who questioned Vin) uncovered his address as being on Rockport Road, down in the suburb of Fern Flats. It's not a horrible area, but it's an old part of town, close to an industrial area and a lot of elderly people live there in old houses, some that are rundown and in need of repair.

I had also found out that he doesn't have a Dad, but I didn't pry into the details. I hadn't known about his sister. None of those factors had made me like him any less.

Messages come through from Sacha: *shopped up a storm, spent too much money, you should have come, girl! Bought you a gorgeous present!*

Aunt Patty's call comes from the bottom of the staircase. "Dinner's ready, Rylee." Her tone is sickly sweet, fake, like she hasn't insulted entire sectors of the population.

I don't reply. I tiptoe out of bed and lock my door. I'm hungry, but I have a granola bar in my purse. I listen to several more shouts from Patty, the rattling of my door handle, exasperated sighs.

But I'm staunch.

I'm not talking to her again.

I'm not leaving my room until Mom and Dad come home.

THE NEXT MORNING I wake to a unique feeling—my stomach is rumbling. The emptiness causes an aching which is from a true and real hunger. Apart from the almond granola bar, I haven't eaten since Aunt Patty made me a hot chocolate mid afternoon.

I forget my vow to barricade myself in my room, and after a hot shower I descend the stairs cautiously, listening for Aunt Patty's movements. The coffee machine is gurgling and the sound of Christmas carols hums in the background.

"Good morning Rylee." She greets me as if there's been no fight, as if I didn't slam her. I ignore her, fixing myself my usual breakfast of yogurt and fruit. "I can do toasted bagels," she says, "and I know you love hot chocolate. By the way, how's your headache today?"

I'm mute. No matter how much I want to retaliate, I bite my tongue. Silence is the best response. It frustrates her.

She carries on, regardless. "I'll do a last minute trip to the grocery store. Your mother left me a list. Do you want to come?" I flick my hair across my shoulder, scooping up my bowl and spoon to take upstairs. "I'm leaving at eleven," she says as I stride off, pleased that I can keep up my performance. Only four or five hours until my parents are back, and then I can be rid of Aunt Patty.

There has been a flurry of snowfall throughout the night, but it's barely hitting the ground now. I go to the window, surveying the street, praying that Mom and Dad's flight can still arrive safely and that roads aren't closed. They have a 90 minute drive from the airport to home.

Something catches my eye on our driveway, something bright and colorful. I squint, trying to focus in on it, then take off down the stairs, pulling off my socks at the front door and padding out in bare feet.

Aunt Patty's voice is hoarse as she yells, "Rylee, Rylee? Where are you going? Rylee, don't leave the door open!"

It's only a few seconds to dash out, pick it up and return inside, but already my toes are freezing, my nose, too.

"What on earth?" Aunt Patty is standing with one hand on her hip, one on the door, as she closes it behind me. "You'll catch a death of cold, young-," she says.

But her words stop abruptly as I hold up the little purple sneaker in front of us. It's wet, the Velcro tape unsecured on this threadbare, tiny generic brand shoe. I turn it over in my hand, the sole revealing it is severely worn down on one side. It's heart breaking.

This is a simple pair of shoes, probably costing no more than five dollars, but they are being worn until they are almost falling apart. I think of Aiden's scuffed up Converse, his holey socks, and this little girl, who limps in a pair of sneakers well past their use by date.

"Wait for me," I say, "I'm coming with you." I hand her the shoe, thinking about how, in his haste to leave, Aiden never stopped to put on Krystal's shoes, that he took her home in her socks.

"I'll wait, dear," Aunt Patty croaks, her voice brittle, "I'll wait, my dear."

AUNT PATTY MAKES SEVERAL attempts at conversation as we head to the mall, but I remain stoic. My mind is churning over. Over and over, relentlessly replaying the scenario, wondering why I offered no resistance, why I didn't stand up for Krystal or Aiden.

My life has been sweet, I know that. My only tragedy has been the passing of my grandmother, who had a stroke, was hospitalized for three months and then died. In a way, we never saw it as a loss, but a blessing that she was free and at peace. Otherwise, I live in comfort, my every need catered for, and most of my wants. Although Dad has deemed a racy red convertible totally unsuitable as my first car, so it's likely I'll get a vehicle which adheres to his high safety standards. I'll probably make a song and dance about it, but it will all be in jest.

I do appreciate my privileged background. I'm aware I've never had to beg and plead for a new phone or a pair of jeans and if I want a manicure or my hair colored or to go to a concert, there is always money on my card. But I'm not a spoilt princess—I have chores to do, I have to feed Bubbles and make my bed and put my clothes away.

I know there are people less fortunate than me—I've donated to the school's food drive when we did a collection for homeless people, and Mom gives all my old clothes to charity shops.

Aunt Patty makes several rounds of the parking lot before finding a spot. The mall is chaos, as it seems everyone is doing last minute shopping. I'm ready to bolt when the car stops, but Aunt Patty clasps my hand.

"Rylee," she says, "I think it's best if we stay together. I don't want you getting lost and it's going to be madness out there."

"I have some things to get," I say, refusing to acknowledge her touch. "I'll meet you back here."

Aunt Patty lets out a deep sigh. "Well, text me when you're ready."

I scramble out of the car, a girl on a mission. What I'm about to do isn't going to erase the words spoken, it's probably not going to change an old lady's prejudice, it's not going to justify my own inertia, but it is going to make one little girl's Christmas a whole lot brighter.

Shopping for someone you don't know, who you've only met once, should be impossibly hard. But I've never had so much fun. I want to buy Krystal everything sparkly and glittery and pink. I want her to have the best Christmas ever.

And I want her brother to, as well.

I have to make amends for the disaster that was yesterday.

Aunt Patty calls me when she's finished her shopping and says she'll wait for me at the car. To spite her, I sit down and have a vanilla latte. I'm not going to rush for her sake. When I eventually arrive back, her face is puckered and tight. That makes me happy; the wait has irritated her. She helps me unload my cart into the trunk, not asking what my purchases are, but I notice her bags seem in excess of the list Mom had left, which consisted mainly of fresh fruit and vegetables, milk and cream.

I'm confident I can continue with my deaf and dumb routine on the journey home, but as soon as we escape the tangle of the parking lot, Aunt Patty's face turns even grimmer.

"I'm afraid I've got some bad news," she says, her eyes focused on the road as the window wipers sweep at the snowflakes that are floating across the windscreen. The snow has gotten a little heavier, and the air conditioned mall was a cruel deception to the true air temperature.

Even with the heat in the car turned up, I can feel the chill factor has dropped considerably since we left the house two and a half hours ago.

"This storm is hitting quicker than was predicted," Aunt Patty says, her leather-gloved hands clenching the wheel as visibility decreases. "I want to get us home as fast as possible. It's going to get dangerous on these roads."

I nod, because I sense a bit of fear in the usually staunch woman, and the build up of traffic indicates everyone has the same idea. There's a tension in the air as we drive home, but it's no longer about our feud, but the shared panic at the deteriorating weather conditions.

It's only as we climb the hill to the safety of our suburb that Aunt Patty's grip relaxes. "Oh my, that's been quite a treacherous journey," she says.

"Yeah, I hope Mom and Dad are going to get through it okay."

That's when Patty's throat tightens. "Rylee, that's what I wanted to tell you," she says, pushing the garage remote as we turn into our driveway, "the bad news."

I turn to her. "Bad news? I thought the bad news was the storm approaching."

"Your Mom rang while you were shopping," she says, sighing as she turns off the engine. "The weather has closed the airport. They won't be able to fly out until tomorrow. And that's with fingers crossed." She reaches out to stroke my hand, but I pull it back quickly as the words take effect: *Mom and Dad won't be home for Christmas morning!*

It takes only a moment to sink in, that my Christmas is not going to be what I've come to know as our family's tradition. Waking early to check my stocking, a breakfast of gingerbread waffles and melted marshmallows and sitting around the tree opening presents, with Dad singing carols off key.

"But they'll be back by lunchtime?" I ask with desperation. I need to find a spark of hope in this dark moment, I need to know that the day won't be completely ruined.

"It's impossible to know." Aunt Patty looks as distraught as I feel. "Laura said she'll call as soon as they know anything. There are going to be thousands of people trying to get home for Christmas. I just hope everyone stays safe." She makes a move to pat my shoulder. I flinch and slam the car door as I storm up to my room.

I'm about to have the worst Christmas ever.

CHAPTER 7

AIDEN

I awake to the smell of coffee and cinnamon scrolls, and though it's tempting to stay under the warm blankets, I peel back the covers and throw a hoodie over my thermal top. Pulling back the drapes reveals a light dusting of snow, enough to make it a fairytale Christmas. The wicked storm that came in last night appears to have dissipated and Christmas is back on track.

Yesterday there were concerns that we'd all be isolated for Christmas, that my grandparents wouldn't be able to cross town to visit, and that the special church lunch would be canceled. But, maybe not.

"I told you I'd make breakfast," I say to Mom, busy amongst the clutter of pots and pans.

"You were sleeping like a baby," she says, with a kiss to my cheek and a ruffle to my hair, "Yesterday must've worn you out."

"Guess it did. I think I zonked out pretty quick." It had been a frantic day at the Christmas tree farm, customers leaving their tree until the last moment. And even with the poor weather forecast, they still turned up, demanding trees. With a couple of the boys unable to make it, I'd had to work in the bitter cold till late. My fingers and toes were intact, but it had taken a steaming hot shower and two cups of cocoa to warm back up. My nose is still the spitting image of Rudolph's. The things we do for extra cash.

"Merry Christmas, Aiden," she says, wrapping herself around me for a hug.

"You too," I say, "here, let me get that," I say, pouring us mugs of hot coffee. I know Mom stayed up late last night, building a gingerbread house for the lunch today. She'd had two frantic days at the market, almost, but not quite selling out of cookies, but it was her candles that did amazing, getting orders for more in the new year. She came home hopeful that she can get ongoing sales for them. "No sign of our little angel?" I ask.

"I hope she sleeps a little longer," she says, "so I can organize a few more things. I think the lunch will be all go."

"Sweet," I say. The church lunch is something Mom helps organize every year, for those who don't have family to share the day with. It started out being focused on kids, but the last couple of years it has grown. It seems there are a lot of lonely people, of all ages, out there during the holiday season.

Mom is an active member of the church, but me—not so much. I debate the existence of an almighty God, always wondering where he was the day Krystal was born and when my Dad had a brain aneurysm. Was there a glut of prayers happening those days, so that ours were missed? Did my irregular church attendance put me at a disadvantage? Do my prayers not count because my beliefs are wavering? I often ponder why my family, especially my Mom, endures such hardship. How can there be a God that cares when Mom's lot seems to be fraught with struggle and suffering?

Krystal wakes up when my grandparents arrive and we have a leisurely morning, watching Krystal delight in opening her presents. The neighbors pop in to share hot drinks and cinnamon scrolls and Krystal's pile of gifts mounts up, her favorite thing a wind-up snow globe that plays Rudolph the Red Nose Reindeer. Grandad keeps pointing at my nose as he sings along, sending Kryssie into fits of giggles.

Our family tradition involves a trip to the cemetery to visit my Dad's grave, but with light rain falling, Mom suggests we do it after lunch when the weather is supposed to improve.

We rally about sorting ourselves, Grandma dressing Krystal in her Red Riding Hood coat. She puts Krystal's sneaker on, then looks around for the other one.

"Where's your other sneaker?" she asks and there's a frantic upturn of the hallway closet, the front porch, under the couch and Kryssie's bedroom.

"When did she wear them last?" Mom asks calmly, amidst the rising panic.

"Yesterday?" I offer.

"No, Mrs Baker was here with her. She never left the house."

"Oh," I say, a lightbulb moment of remembrance. "We went to see the lights. It's probably in my trunk with her scooter." I don my beanie and a jacket and race out to my car. A search comes up with the scooter, but no purple sneaker.

I'd left Rylee's house in a hurry, grabbing my sister and her shoes like wildfire was approaching. I have purposely tried to erase the memory of Aunt Patty's scathing words, her disrespect towards special children, her narrow minded view on those she considers beneath her. Unfortunately, it's not the first time I've encountered that kind of discrimination. People can fear what they don't know. I'm not usually affected by it now—for ten years I've seen the stares, heard the whispers, experienced the exclusion—because she's different, because she's not normal. But it doesn't mean it hurts any less when I hear it.

It's heart breaking, but as Mom says *It is what it is*. Krystal's life is precious to us, her very existence seen as a blessing. And as we know, in the case of my Dad, life can be taken at anytime, cruelly, unfairly, seemingly without rhyme or reason.

Mom finds Krystal's boots but she refuses to put them on—it's the purple sneakers or nothing—her attachment to them has bewildered us for the past year. An identical pink pair has been rejected numerous times, no amount of trickery can persuade her to put them on. No one is sure of what or why, but we do worry about what will happen when her feet grow too big.

Grandad says sneakers are unnecessary, gives her an extra pair of socks and carries her. I'm thinking I must have dropped the sneaker somewhere between Rylee's house and the car. I know it seems silly but I'm going to have to go on a search for it; hopefully no one has put it in the trash.

Grandma says it's a sign from God that the weather clears just as we leave for the church lunch. I question that—preferring to believe that the cold front has moved east, as was predicted in the weather forecast. The glamor of a white Christmas is just that, in real life it disrupts everyone's plans, but it makes for pretty pictures.

The lunch is a shared effort by the community with food donated and cooked, and the volunteers, Mom and myself included, help to serve up plates as people file in from the cold. Everyone is welcome without judgment, no one turned away, even those who arrive in new cars, wearing designer coats. I guess loneliness comes in many forms, and it makes me appreciate that family and happiness means more than having buckets of money.

With the weather being poor, it was thought that there might be less people through today, but the opposite occurs and we're busier than ever. Grandad and I, who are on roast potatoes and green beans respectively, are onto our last trays. Portions are diminishing as we see the queue snakes towards the door.

"We'll be having bread and jam for lunch," Grandpa jokes, as it's obvious there won't be enough food for the volunteers. "Ma'am, one potato or two?" he asks the woman in line.

"None, thank you," she says, and I look up, immediately recognizing the voice. How could I not? It's one that is embedded bone-deep, the cruelty of its words a little too raw.

"Carb free diet?" Grandad chuckles, winking at the poker face of Aunt Patty.

Grandad is a right old charmer—and her face softens, but only for a moment.

"It's this boy I'd like to steal. For a moment." Her eyes pierce mine, rheumy, bloodshot, dull. "If I may."

Grandad looks at me; if he's surprised, he doesn't show it. "Go ahead. I think I can mange the beans, as well." Another hearty chuckle.

I'm stuck holding the ladle, wanting to deny this horrible woman the chance to apologize, almost about to say, "I'm busy and not interested in what you have to say," but it is Christmas, and Christmas is about love and peace and joy to the world. Apparently.

"Sure," I say, wiping my hands on my Santa apron. I follow Aunt Patty over to the entrance, repositioning my Santa hat. You can't be unjolly wearing a Santa hat, surely.

I take a deep breath, curious as to what she has to say, internally muttering *Peace on earth, peace on earth,* as a reminder to myself.

"It's not the appropriate place to apologize, I realize that," Aunt Patty tries to sound authoritative and in control, but her trembling hands, her hollowed cheeks, her tight lips reveal her vulnerability. "But I need your help, Aiden. Please help me."

And without warning, she collapses into my arms.

CHAPTER 8

RYLEE

I cry my eyes out when Mom rings me a short while later. She sounds so far away and the reality sinks in that I'm stuck with Aunt Patty. All avenues of getting home have been investigated, but Mom says that they're hopeful flights will resume in the morning and they'll be home by mid afternoon.

"You'll be fine sweetheart," she reassures, "and I've already rearranged plans, so we'll have our big Christmas dinner in the evening. Everything will essentially be the same, just four or five hours later than normal."

I try to stifle my tears then, because saying it like that makes me feel like I'm being a baby. And if I stay in bed until noon, I'll hardly have to see Aunt Patty and it will only be a short wait till their return.

There's a knock on my door, and as I've locked it again, there's a rattle and pull of the handle.

"Rylee, dear? I've put your shopping outside your door here." Aunt Patty waits for my response, but I won't succumb. "And Bubbles is hungry. You might want to come down and feed him, dear."

I leap off of the bed, waiting by the door until I'm sure she's left. I feel guilty at making her carry the four big shopping bags from the garage up to my room. Plus, she brought in all the groceries. Aunt Patty is in her seventies, and she's fit and healthy, but there's not much to her, and I really should have helped.

I creep down into the kitchen, where Bubbles is circling his food bowl. I fill his dish, and as Aunt Patty seems to be elsewhere, make myself a sandwich and sit down at the table, scrolling through my phone. Everyone seems to be having a fabulous day, Sacha is with her family, Casey is wrapping presents, Bree is baking, Ailyah is sitting around a log fire.

No one wants to know about my misery, having Christmas with an evil Great Aunt while my parents are a thousand miles away. I snap a photo of Bubbles, give him a reindeer filter and post that. It quickly gathers many likes, and everyone believes I'm having the time of my life.

Armed with scissors and sticky tape, I take myself back upstairs in a hurry when I hear Aunt Patty's slippers scuff along the floor. Apart from a little Santa jacket I bought for Bubbles—something he'll never wear, but it was too cute not to buy—the purchases are all for Krystal. I have no idea when I'll see her or how I'll get them to her, but I'm sure Mom or Sacha will be able to help. Of all my friends, Sacha is the only one of us who has her licence and own car. I'll be getting mine in the summer.

I open the box of the glittery purple sneakers I bought. They're a good brand and will be way more comfortable for her. I felt a bit silly in the store, holding the old shoe up to compare size, but with the label worn off, it was the only way to make sure they'll fit. And just in case I'm wrong, I bought the next size up as well, so she can grow into them.

There are so many cute things for girls, that I kind of did go crazy. I figured if Krystal likes purple shoes, she'll like purple socks and purple t-shirts and purple hair bands and purple gloves. Yeah, I went overboard, but as I wrap them up, it brings a joy to my heart.

"Oh, there you are," Aunt Patty clears her throat, standing at the door that I forgot to shut, offering a mug of hot chocolate. "Thought you could do with this."

I'm holding a little soft unicorn toy—very purple—and find it hard to scowl, even though that's what I want to do.

"Thanks," I mumble, because her hot chocolates are the best, and she takes that as a sign to enter, putting it down on my bedside table.

I keep my head down, cutting the paper to the right size and folding it around the unicorn.

"So many lovely things," she says, nodding at the pile still unwrapped.

"They're for Krystal." I enunciate her name with deliberate sarcasm.

Aunt Patty clears her throat again. "Rylee...I'm sorry, I-"

I cut in with brutality. "You're sorry you're prejudiced against people with disabilities or you're sorry you're such a mean, hurtful person?" Aunt Patty's eyes glaze and her jaw slackens; it's like I've physically attacked her, and for a moment I think she might collapse, but she crosses her arms tightly over her chest and retreats like a scared cat. Or Bubbles when confronted by the neighbor's little dog.

The last thing I wrap is a packet of socks and the *One Million cologne*. It's for Aiden, but I'm under no illusion that I'll actually give it to him, that I'll be brave enough to. It's been twenty four hours since he fled my house, and it burns with embarrassment that he had to.

I'm pretty sure he hates me as much as I hate Aunt Patty.

CHAPTER 9

AIDEN

The Reverend materializes from nowhere, as does Mr Biggs, who a moment ago, had carried in a box of fruit pies. A chair is pulled over, and with their help we get Aunt Patty on to it, her legs as wobbly as jello. A glass of water is produced by Mom, who has abandoned her hostess position.

She kneels next to Aunt Patty, feeling her forehead temperature, like she's a nurse. "Ma'am are you okay?" she asks, taking a hold of her hand, now checking her pulse.

Patty sips on the water, and clearly uncomfortable with the attention, attempts to stand. "I'm fine, really I'm fine."

"Ma'am, you collapsed into my son's arms," Mom says gently, "I suggest you're not fine at all. Take a moment to rest, please."

Patty looks from Mom to me, and back to Mom. "You're Aiden's mother?"

Mom looks puzzled. "You know Aiden?" She sends a frown in my direction, then has a lightbulb moment, "Oh, from the Christmas tree farm?"

Patty sips more water, but her voice is croaky. "No, he knows my great niece, Rylee. They had a nice time at the Winter Dance."

Mom's eyebrows draw closer just a fraction, but enough for me to know her brain cells are rapidly connecting the dots. I never told her about dancing with Rylee; I didn't need to. Harry had opened his big mouth and blabbed, "Mrs B, did Aiden tell you he danced? With a girl? With his arms around her?" All said with delicious melodrama.

Maybe because my face had burned fire engine red, Mom had simply nodded and smiled, and focused on Harry's dancing success, his story embellished with every retelling.

"You said you needed my help?" I say, confused as to how Patty has found me here. Has she tracked me down? Or has she got a flat tire, or is her car stuck and she has come here randomly and recognized me? "Is everything all right?"

Patty lets out a quivery sob, the stern face has crumbled to one of fear and distress. She shakes her head over and over before taking a gulp of air. "I've ruined her Christmas, and her parents are stuck because of the airport closures, and my dear wee girl is heartbroken." Her eyes connect with me fleetingly, "And she's very angry with me," she whispers, as if she knows that I'll understand.

"Oh, that's terrible," Mom says, "the storm has certainly disrupted a lot of travel plans. What a shame." She comforts the old lady with a hand on her shoulder. "Now what can Aiden do to help?" she asks, volunteering my services.

Now Patty looks me directly in the eye, the plea from the bottom of her heart. "If Aiden and Krystal could visit, I'm sure it would make her day."

Mom blinks rapidly, like a bug just flew into her eye. "Krystal?"

I know she's confused, but I don't have time to explain. My heart rate is increasing manically. The thought of Rylee being unhappy and distraught and alone on Christmas Day, her parents far away, tears at me.

"Is she home alone?" I ask.

Patty nods. "Will you come with me? Please?" The bitterness and superiority has dissipated and all I see is a lonely, sad, scared old woman.

"Mom? Can I? Can I take Kryssie? She's eaten, hasn't she?" Krystal and the children were the first ones fed, she's had her gift from Santa, there's music and carols and dessert to come, but it won't matter if she misses that. Rylee can't be alone on Christmas Day.

Mom shrugs, then nods, all flustered as she's not quite sure what's going on, but I can see she trusts me, that she knows it's something that has to be done. She bundles up Krystal in her coat, and puts her into my arms.

"I expect the full story later," she says, kissing my cheek,

I duly nod, and Mom assists Aunt Patty, who has miraculously regained full strength.

Patty's car is a Jaguar, it's the flashiest and most luxurious car I've ever ridden in. It purrs along, as its name suggests.

It doesn't feel like we're driving in silence because the conversation going on in my head is so loud. My heart rate is at ridiculously high levels and I can't seem to calm myself down. Rylee's happiness is all that seems to matter. Instead of reaching out to her, I punished her for Aunt Patty's wrongdoings. I lumped them together.

I'm no better than Aunt Patty.

Patty drives into the garage.

"I think I dropped her shoe the other day," I say, when Aunt Patty looks down at Krystal's socks, as I lift her from the backseat.

"Rylee found it," Patty says.

"Oh good, it's her favorite pair. She wouldn't wear her boots today, it's the purple sneakers or nothing." I feel the need to justify why a little girl is only wearing socks on one of the coldest days of the year.

But there's no rebuttal, just Aunt Patty affectionately touching Krystal's chin and saying, "Let's go see the Santa Sleigh, shall we?"

CHAPTER 10

RYLEE

I hear Aunt Patty's voice, figuring she's going mad talking to herself. A little while ago she said she was going to church, probably to repent her sins and try to save her wicked soul, so I'm surprised she's back so soon. Usually the service goes for over an hour, longer if there's lots of singing.

I sneaked downstairs when I saw her car go out, feeling a little guilty to see all the work she'd done. She'd stuffed the turkey, cut up vegetables, baked a pie, folded napkins, set the table, filled the stockings. All while I was curled up in bed, feeling sorry for myself.

Mom's text came at eleven, just after Aunt Patty left—there was a short delay, but they were about to board the plane, so all going well, they'd be home at about five. With that in mind, and the fact that I'm bored, I've dressed and styled my hair and put on makeup. I want to be pretty for Mom and Dad.

But I'm still not leaving my room.

I hear Aunt Patty's footsteps on the stairs, and in case she's about to knock, I ready myself by sitting on the side of my bed.

"Rylee, dear?" Her voice is tentative, a little breathless, "Rylee? There's someone here to see you. Will you come out, dear?"

I'm instantly curious. Who would be here to see me? I cross to the window. There are no cars out the front. It has to be a ploy.

"I'm busy," I call back. It could be our neighbor, Mr Hammond. He's usually at our Christmas lunch, though I doubt that he'd particularly want to see me.

"Please, dear." There's desperation in her voice, and for a split second I feel mean, but I remain stubborn, unmuting the movie that I'm watching on my tablet.

There's no rattling of the door handle, so I assume she's given up on me, which surprisingly, doesn't make me feel triumphant, but disappointed.

I roll over onto my side, propping the screen against a pillow, when there's a knock on the door, a loud, crisp knock. Maybe Mr Hammond *does* want to see me. I sit up again, anticipating his deep, gravelly greeting.

"Rylee?" In shock, I spring off the bed, the next words confirming my worst fears and best dreams all in one, "Rylee, it's Aiden. Can I come in?"

I bound across to my dressing table, checking my hair in the mirror. Aiden Barrett is outside my bedroom door! My heart rate escalates as I reposition a wayward strand of hair.

"Rylee? Are you in there?"

The weight of my immaturity reveals itself in that moment. I am locked up in my room, like a precocious princess, refusing to come out until my parents come home.

On Christmas Day.

I'm pathetic.

I open the door, making him stumble, like he had his ear up against it.

"Uh, sorry," he says, as he falls into my room. We spontaneously take hold of each other, hands on each other's forearms. "Oh, you are here." He grins, not releasing his grip, even though we're standing independently now.

"Yep." A tingle is running through me, his touch making a kaleidoscope of colors explode in my brain. Our eyes lock; an intensity that has taken my breath away. It seems impossible to take our eyes off of each other.

How much time passes?

I don't know.

All I know is that I feel warm, comforted, happy.

And I haven't been happy in days.

"Merry Christmas, Rylee," he says and he pulls me in for a hug, his arms wrapping around me like he doesn't want me to escape. He smells good—nothing definable—just good.

"Merry Christmas, Aiden," I reply, my nose snuggling into his black puffer jacket.

He releases me, his eyes focused on my lips. He blinks himself out of the stare. "Uh, Krystal's downstairs."

"Is she?" I'm at a loss, not understanding how he got here, and astonished that Krystal could be downstairs with Aunt Patty. I need to save her.

Pulling him by the hand, we take the stairs two at a time. The living room smells of cinnamon and gingerbread and I survey the situation: Aunt Patty sitting demurely on the couch, within arms length of Krystal, who is once again enthralled with the Santa Sleigh.

"What's going on?"

"Merry Christmas, Rylee dear," Aunt Patty says.

I ignore her, releasing Aiden's hand to kneel next to Krystal. Her eyes light up, her smile broadens, her fingers try to point at Santa going round and round and round. There's so much joy, so much contentment.

"Rylee. Aiden." Our names are spoken as a command, and Aunt Patty's watering eyes direct us to sit across from her. Whether it's common courtesy or respect, we feel compelled to follow her instruction.

Aiden leaves no space between us, we're sitting on the couch as if we're squeezed into a crowded subway train. I place my hands in my lap and my heart flips when Aiden covers his hand over mine. Another spine tingling moment.

Aunt Patty clears her throat, but instead of a booming, authoritative voice, a feeble, fragile sound emerges. "They wouldn't let me keep him."

There's a confused silence, an eeriness from words that have no meaning to us, but spoken from a place of utter powerlessness, her vulnerability viciously exposed. And then, a whimper barely escapes her mouth, "I wasn't allowed to hold him."

Aiden and I are statues, frozen, unsure of what she is implying but as tears dribble down her cheeks, as her nostrils quiver and her chin twitches, we face each other, his hand squeezing down more firmly on mine.

"Aunt Patty?" I whisper, all my resentment and hatred vanishes. "Who? *Who?*"

Aunt Patty dabs delicately with a folded lilac handkerchief, her eyes, her cheeks, her nose. "He wasn't normal. They told me I couldn't keep him. He had a..." The pause causes Aiden and I to lean forward to hear her whisper, "A deformity." She wipes a new tear, her voice robotic, "My husband said to take him away."

I reluctantly leave Aiden's grasp, leaping to Aunt Patty's side, kneeling on the floor. "*Your husband?*"

I'm reeling. Aunt Patty is supposed to be a spinster, her career ambitions and single mindedness her only priority. Her life was about building a sporting goods empire that supplied schools all across the country. Those gym mats you bounced on in elementary school, those soccer balls, those basketball hoops—chances are they were all provided by her company. There was no time, or need for relationships.

That's what I'd been told.

"Thomas Harrington." She almost chokes on the name, her contempt undisguised. "The third." Her chin trembles again, she tightens her mouth, refusing to succumb to more tears. "He wouldn't name him. Didn't give him a name."

"*You had a baby?*"

Aunt Patty looks down at me, her eyes closing in shame. She grips my hand, and I reciprocate, squeezing back. This usually regal looking woman looks broken, her pain is buried deep.

Her inhale is wavering, her hold on me tightens. "I had a son." It feels like she has never uttered those words out loud. "I had a son."

"Aunt Patty," I say, but I'm inadequate. I don't know how to comfort. I have so many questions—*Do Mom and Dad know? Where's the baby now? What happened to her husband?*

Aiden draws his long legs beneath him, as he kneels beside me, his arm around me, like he knows I need him. And I do.

"Did you name him?" he asks gently.

Aunt Patty's chin trembles. "Simon," she says, and her eyes brighten, the drooping lids lifting and widening. "I called him Simon."

And that seems to be the validation she needs to tell her story. The verbalization of her son's name allows her to acknowledge her carefully guarded secret. Her son, born with multiple deformities, whisked off to a 'special place' where he would be cared for by specialists, her husband knowing best. Like a dutiful wife, she had been forced to oblige, her choice taken away.

Along with her heart, her mind, her soul.

A breakdown had followed, and her privileged world snatched from her when Thomas Harrington divorced her. Alone, she'd found her coping mechanism—work, hard, hard work. She used it to forget the memory of the baby she had never held.

"What happened to Simon, Aunt Patty?" I ask.

"He died at four months old."

"I'm sorry for your loss," Aiden says, his compassion heart-warming.

Aunt Patty heaves out a sob, and pats Aiden's hand. "No, no, no, don't be sorry for me," she says, "I'm the one who is sorry. I saw your beautiful sister, a girl who I can see is loved for who she is. And I was angry. Angry with myself. I wished I'd been stronger. I wish I'd fought for my son." Aunt Patty's tears are streaming. "I said hurtful, hurtful words. Unforgivable words. I can see your sister means the world to you, and I felt jealous and robbed and resentful—you value Krystal's life, but I never got to give my son that chance. Your strength is admirable, young man."

Aiden's cheeks turns as red as his nose. "She's my sister, and I love her," he says simply. He turns to watch Krystal—we all do—her fascination with the Santa Sleigh hasn't dimmed. His voice softens. "You know, I think they were different times back then. Even now, some people think Krystal belongs in a care facility."

Aunt Patty looks overwhelmed. She clutches her chin between her hands, shaking her head. "I don't deserve your kind words. None of them." She looks at me. "And you're right, my dear, I'm a horrible person. I've humiliated myself. I ask for your forgiveness. Both of you, please forgive me."

CHAPTER 11

AIDEN

I'm not sure how I came to be an integral part of Aunt Patty's staggering revelation, but I suddenly find myself hugging an old lady and the girl of my dreams, at the same time. It isn't the worst thing that can happen to a boy on Christmas Day. There's a mingling of rose and vanilla fragrances, and my body temperature soars.

Nobody seems to want to be the first to release, and it's my beautiful sister who makes us unbind.

The sound she makes is undecipherable, but there's an attempted clap as something has made her excitable. Her attention is off of the Santa Sleigh and she's spotted a swaying of baubles on the tree. A tabby colored cat darts out, disturbing decorations and gift wrapped boxes.

"Bubbles!" Aunt Patty is on her feet. "Naughty cat," she scolds, but Bubbles is long gone.

Krystal makes her way to the tree, a glittering ball enticing her. I'm by her side in a flash, keen to avoid a falling tree.

"Hey, little fairy," Rylee joins me and bends down to her level, "how about we take this coat off of you? Because I've got a little something for you."

"It is hot in here" I say, feeling flushed from having her next to me. I jump in to assist with the unbuttoning of the coat, which is totally unnecessary; there are three buttons. I remove my own jacket and Aunt Patty is right there, acting like the coat attendant, taking them away. It feels a little mixed up.

"I did a little shopping yesterday," Rylee says, her smile coy. "Wait here, and I'll be back in a second." She disappears and Aunt Patty returns with a tray of delicious looking snacks.

"I know you must be hungry," she says, "you've obviously had a busy morning helping at the church and I've taken you away from your lunch."

"I'm fine," I say, though I am starving. A familiar smell of gingerbread is starting to permeate the room.

"Nonsense," Aunt Patty says. "There's plenty of food here, and I want you to invite your mother and your grandparents here when they finish at church." There's an authority in her voice that I dare not question and it seems an eternity ago that she broke down and poured her heart out to us.

I make the phone call to Mom, who asks me ten times if Krystal is all right, because I've forgotten to bring her bag with her. Aunt Patty is feeding her a star shaped cookie, crumbs dropping to the floor, so I dive across to pick them up.

Aunt Patty waves me away with a smile. "It's only crumbs, it can be cleaned later." Already she looks younger, radiant, her skin smoother, her eyes clearer, released from her unimaginable secret.

Rylee comes racing back into the room, her arms loaded with two large shopping bags. My heart rejoices and sinks at the same time. I'm pleased for Krystal, but I'm crushed that I have nothing to offer in return. She is also holding up Krystal's lost shoe.

"I found this in the driveway," she says.

I point to Krystal's socks. "You're a lifesaver," I say, "She refuses to wear anything but the purple sneakers."

"Oh?" Rylee looks surprised. "Oh." She bites down on her lower lip. "I thought they were her only pair, and-"

She stops mid-sentence, and I'm mortified by the thought that Rylee thinks we're poor, *that poor*, that we can't afford decent shoes for my sister. It's awkward. I glance at my own socks, black, kind of new, no holes, almost like I have to make a point.

"Rylee couldn't help herself," Aunt Patty says, delicately wiping around Krystal's mouth with a napkin, "I'm sure this little one is going to love them." She affectionately strokes Krystal's hair.

"I hope you don't mind," Rylee says, her voice tiny, like she senses I'm angry at her, that she's embarrassed me.

I don't want her to feel like that. I don't want her to know that we are financially worlds apart, but being offended and overly sensitive isn't going to achieve anything. I can hear Mom's voice loud in my head: *It is what it is.*

Rylee has a gift, or from the look of it, lots of gifts for Krystal. Who am I to deny her the pleasure of giving? She's opening her heart to my sister, and I'm grateful for that.

"I'm blown away that you would even think about buying her a gift," I say, "thank you."

We stare at each other for a moment, and my foolish eyes are watering and Rylee leans into me, embracing me, her hair tickling my cheek. I don't want to let her go, I want to scoop her up and swing her in my arms and kiss her lips, and relive the Winter Dance all over again.

But Krystal is waving her arms in anticipation of the shiny packages, and Rylee hands her a present. Krystal's unwrapping speed is much like her scootering—snail pace. It takes a lot of restraint not to pull the bow and tape off for her.

Krystal delights in each and every gift—the soft toy, the clothes, the candy. Rylee brings out the last two boxes reluctantly. "She might not like these," she says, "but I thought they were cute. Maybe we can persuade her to put them on." She raises her eyebrows with a grimace, but I love her optimism. In fact there are a lot of things I love about Rylee Martin.

Krystal giggles as she rips at the paper. Aunt Patty assists with the opening of the lid. She holds up a pair of glittery purple sneakers, a little flashy for my liking, but Krystal's eyes light up.

"Aren't these pretty?" Aunt Patty says, in super sales mode. "Won't these look pretty on your feet?"

Krystal is looking down at her socks, her fingers pointing. My heart is pounding because I'm still not hopeful that Rylee can convince her to wear them.

But I play along. "Aren't you lucky, Kryssie? Aren't they the coolest shoes?"

Rylee kneels beside her, pulling on the elasticated laces. "Look at these! I bet they'll look good on you." She wiggles Krystal's toes, making her laugh.

Krystal looks across to her old sneaker, in amongst the giftwrap. I see Rylee's face drop in disappointment.

"Hey, let's try these on, Kryssie," I say, picking up the purple fleecy mittens, "they look nice and warm." Using gestures, I signal for Rylee to put the new shoes on her, while I'm distracting her with the mittens and Aunt Patty puts the fairy wings on, and then gathers up the discarded wrapping, discreetly taking the old shoe with it.

"Oh, so pretty," Rylee says, touching Krystal's hair braids. "Shall we look in the mirror?"

I take Kryssie by one hand and Rylee takes the other and we walk her out into the hallway, but her gait seems different, likes she's taking giant steps. I fear the shoes are hurting her. Rylee directs us to a full length mirror next to the coat stand.

"Look at your new gloves," I say, making her clap her hands together, "and your wings." I make her spin around, trying to take the focus off of her feet. Krystal smiles, then she looks down to her shoes. There's a moment of confusion as she stares at the unfamiliar footwear, as if we haven't fooled her one bit. She bends down and touches them, and I'm expecting some agitation, but she marches on the spot and says something that sounds like *shoe*. Or it could be *new*.

Then she stands up and I can't believe what I'm seeing. She puts her arms around Rylee, who is crouching next to her, and gives her a hug. My eyes well up—again.

"I think she's a fan of those shoes," I say, trying to keep my voice from breaking. "That's her thank you hug."

"You're welcome, little fairy," Rylee says, snuggling into her and rubbing their noses together. A tear drips down my cheek and I hastily wipe it away. A hand presses on my shoulder and Aunt Patty smiles at me.

"I've got some hot chocolate on the stove," she says, "Come through for a mug?" Rylee and I nod, and Aunt Patty reaches down to take Krystal's hand. Krystal walks likes she's a new giraffe just finding her feet.

"Hey...Aiden," Rylee says, as I'm about to follow them through to the dining area.

"She looks so cute," I say.

"Yeah, she's adorable."

I'm thinking, *So are you.* But I say, "I can't thank you enough."

Rylee smiles mischievously, she tilts her head a little, her eyes roll up to the ceiling.

"What?"

"Up there." Her eyes roll up again.

I see a high timber ceiling. There's a lot of exquisite wood in this house, my eyes drawn to the staircase which is a fine example.

"It's nice," I say.

Rylee frowns, then she laughs. It's glorious, even though I get the distinct feeling she's laughing *at* me. "There," she says, pointedly showing me a bunch of decorative greenery over the dining room door frame. "Do you know what that is?"

Heat sweeps upwards from my neck, right through my cheeks, up to the top of my head. I've never felt more dense in my life. My heart rate accelerates and I know I need to make a joke of this, or I'll never live it down. With a deadpan face, I slowly shake my head from side to side.

"No?" Rylee looks surprised. I keep shaking my head. "You haven't heard of the tradition of mistletoe?"

"Mistle what?"

"Toe. Mistle*toe*."

"Nope. Tell me." I inch a fraction closer to her, looking up as if I need to get a better view of it. "What's the tradition?"

"You really don't know?" She's trying not to sound bewildered, but I'm doing an incredible job of keeping a straight face. "Like you've never heard what you should do if you're caught under the mistletoe?"

I shrug. "Can you show me?"

"Well, it's...well, " she stutters, looking awkward and uncomfortable, "well, if you meet someone under the mistletoe, tradition says you're supposed to-" She stops abruptly, her cheeks blushing now, and in one swift, unexpected move, she goes up on tip toes and her lips meet mine.

Taken by surprise, my arms automatically encircle her, pulling her in close, our kiss sweet and soft and perfect. I don't want it to end, having Rylee in my arms is a dream come true, a Christmas wish I never thought would happen.

As our lips part, she finishes her sentence, "As I was saying, tradition says you're supposed to kiss, and..."

She has more to say, but I don't want to hear it. My lips graze her forehead, then my nose brushes hers, and then, *it's my turn to kiss her.*

EPILOGUE

AIDEN

IF I HAD A WAVERING belief about life being unfair and unjust and nobody looking out for me and my family, in one extraordinary day, it was all erased. You see, the smell of gingerbread in the Martin house didn't come from baking—it came from my Mom's candles which lined the dining room table. Aunt Patty had bought a bunch of them from the Christmas markets. When Rylee's Mom and Dad came home later that evening, they fell in love with them. They are commissioning Mom to make and supply one of their giftware stores in town.

And Aunt Patty, she's becoming involved in the children's charity, putting her business skills to use for fundraising for children with special needs.

As for Krystal, trying to remove her new shoes was a nightmare. The first night no one even tried to. Now she sleeps with them at the end of her bed. She has a new toy in her room too—Aunt Patty gave her the Santa Sleigh from Switzerland. She said it was a shame to only have it on show for a few weeks of the year, when it could be giving joy to a little girl every single day.

And Rylee, well she calls me her Christmas boyfriend, and jokes that I better not forget our anniversary date. I doubt that's going to happen.

You see, I'm not Rylee's Christmas boyfriend, I plan on being her forever boyfriend.

THE END

THANK YOU FOR READING my book and I hope it brought you a moment of joy. If you enjoyed it, please consider leaving a review or rating or shouting out on social media! And do check out my other books where you'll find all the sweetness of falling in love for the first time! ♡

CONNECT WITH ME!

Check out my Amazon page here:

https://www.amazon.com/author/kyliekey

Join my newsletter here:

http://eepurl.com/dKX-A2

Other books by Kylie Key

COVINGTON PREP: THE GIRLS WE LOVE

https://www.amazon.com/gp/product/B09KXFF5VM

The Tomboy - Taylor & Max

The Bookworm - Millie & Tennessee

The Kid Sister - Sierra & Cullen

The Heiress - Elisha & Phoenix

The Queen Bee - Bianca & Raine

The Celebrity - Tamsyn & Sloan

The Rebel - Valencia & Jade

The Wallflower - Izzy & Paris

THE YOUNG LOVE SERIES

https://www.amazon.com/gp/product/B08454JT1D

The Songs We Sing - Ella & Damon

The Path We Take - Dominique & Malachi

The Lies We Tell - Trieste & Felix

The Hearts We Break - Selina & Cole

The Dreams We Share - Ainsley & Logan

The Choices We Make - Damon

THE RIVER VALLEY HIGH BOYFRIEND SERIES

https://www.amazon.com/gp/product/B087KW9P14

My High School Fake Boyfriend - Maddie & Peyton

My High School Billionaire Boyfriend - Bella & Jack

My High School Rebel Boyfriend - Harper & Mitchell

My High School Royal Boyfriend - Blaire & Alexander

My High School Valentine Boyfriend - Shay & Finn

My High School Quarterback Boyfriend - Tanchia & Dean

My High School Secret Boyfriend - Saffron & Kyran

My High School Christmas Boyfriend - Rylee & Aiden

SWEET CRUSHES SERIES

https://www.amazon.com/dp/B0CW17BRVT

His Christmas Angel - Angelina & Chase

Cafe Crush - Evie & Taine

YATOLST
christmas

Made in the USA
Monee, IL
02 January 2025

75911334R00049